Jack

AND THE

Beanstalk

A PARRAGON BOOK

Published by
Parragon Books,
Unit 13–17, Avonbridge Trading Estate,
Atlantic Road, Avonmouth, Bristol BS11 9QD

Produced by
The Templar Company plc,
Pippbrook Mill, London Road, Dorking, Surrey RH4 1JE

Edited by Stephanie Laslett

Designed by Mark Kingsley-Monks

Printed and bound in Italy

ISBN 0-75250-944-6

Jack
— AND THE —
Beanstalk

Retold by Stephanie Laslett
Illustrated by David Anstey

‖ •PARRAGON• ‖

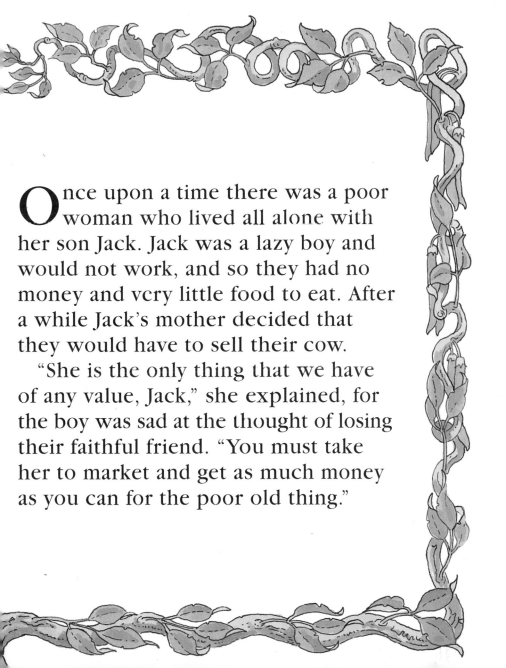

Once upon a time there was a poor woman who lived all alone with her son Jack. Jack was a lazy boy and would not work, and so they had no money and very little food to eat. After a while Jack's mother decided that they would have to sell their cow.

"She is the only thing that we have of any value, Jack," she explained, for the boy was sad at the thought of losing their faithful friend. "You must take her to market and get as much money as you can for the poor old thing."

So the next day Jack set off for market, but he hadn't gone far when he met an old pedlar.

"I like the look of your cow," said the man. "Will you sell her?"

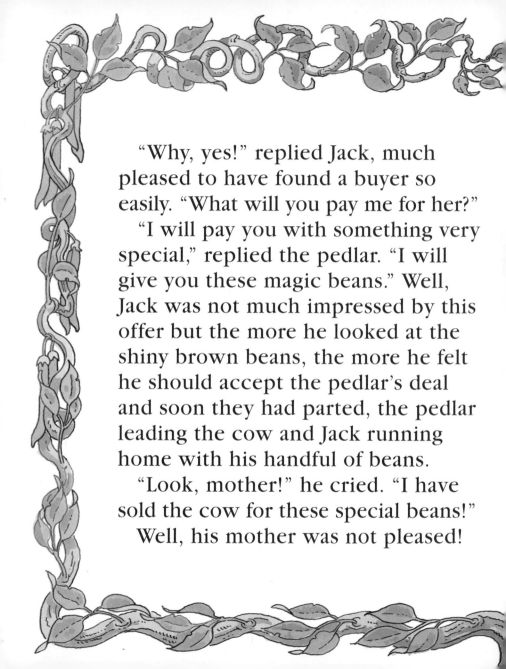

"Why, yes!" replied Jack, much pleased to have found a buyer so easily. "What will you pay me for her?"

"I will pay you with something very special," replied the pedlar. "I will give you these magic beans." Well, Jack was not much impressed by this offer but the more he looked at the shiny brown beans, the more he felt he should accept the pedlar's deal and soon they had parted, the pedlar leading the cow and Jack running home with his handful of beans.

"Look, mother!" he cried. "I have sold the cow for these special beans!"

Well, his mother was not pleased!

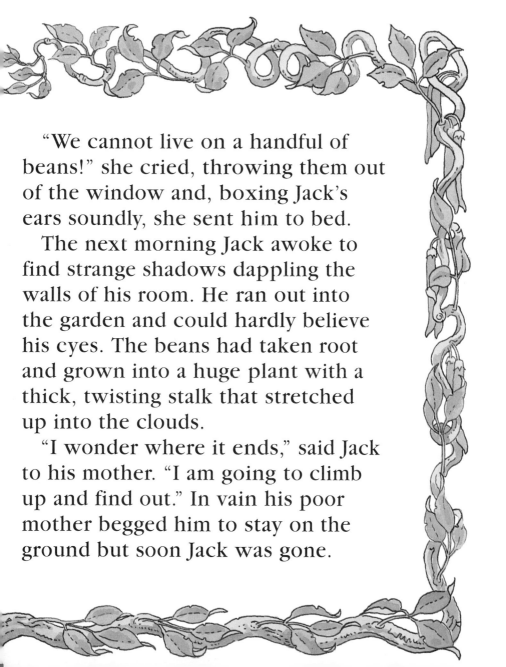

"We cannot live on a handful of beans!" she cried, throwing them out of the window and, boxing Jack's ears soundly, she sent him to bed.

The next morning Jack awoke to find strange shadows dappling the walls of his room. He ran out into the garden and could hardly believe his eyes. The beans had taken root and grown into a huge plant with a thick, twisting stalk that stretched up into the clouds.

"I wonder where it ends," said Jack to his mother. "I am going to climb up and find out." In vain his poor mother begged him to stay on the ground but soon Jack was gone.

At the top of the stalk Jack was astonished to find a fine castle among the clouds. He was hungry but when he knocked on the door for some food, he did not get a warm welcome.

"You must go away at once!" cried the old woman. "My husband is a giant!" But soon crafty Jack had wheedled his way inside the kitchen.

No sooner had he sat down than he felt the floor wobble beneath his chair. "My husband is coming!" cried the woman. "He will surely gobble you up if he finds you here. You must hide at once!"

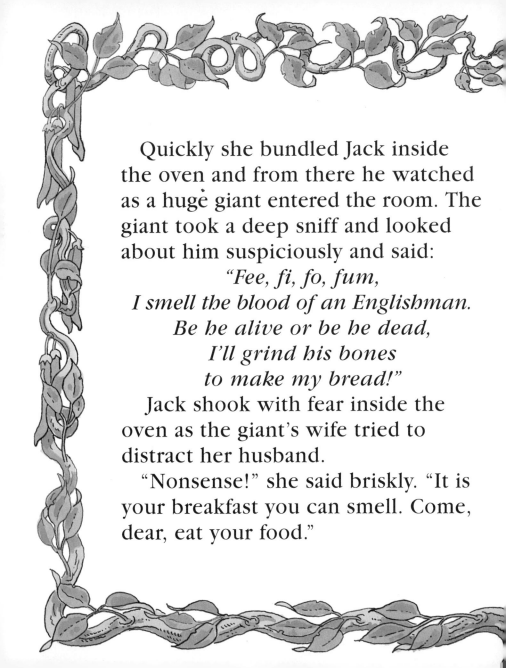

Quickly she bundled Jack inside
the oven and from there he watched
as a huge giant entered the room. The
giant took a deep sniff and looked
about him suspiciously and said:

"Fee, fi, fo, fum,
I smell the blood of an Englishman.
Be he alive or be he dead,
I'll grind his bones
to make my bread!"

Jack shook with fear inside the
oven as the giant's wife tried to
distract her husband.

"Nonsense!" she said briskly. "It is
your breakfast you can smell. Come,
dear, eat your food."

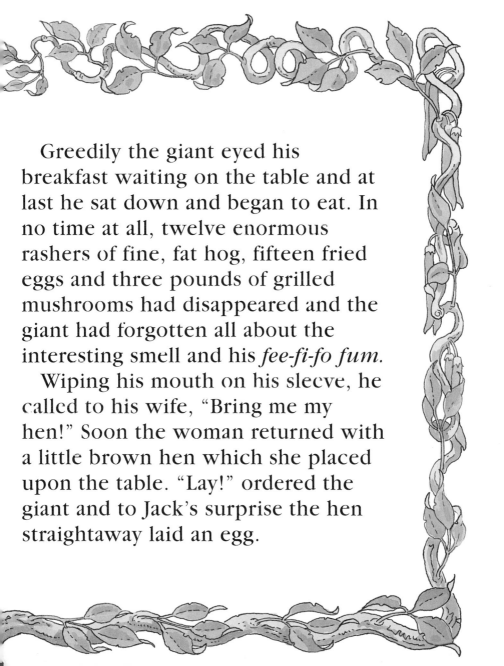

Greedily the giant eyed his breakfast waiting on the table and at last he sat down and began to eat. In no time at all, twelve enormous rashers of fine, fat hog, fifteen fried eggs and three pounds of grilled mushrooms had disappeared and the giant had forgotten all about the interesting smell and his *fee-fi-fo fum*.

Wiping his mouth on his sleeve, he called to his wife, "Bring me my hen!" Soon the woman returned with a little brown hen which she placed upon the table. "Lay!" ordered the giant and to Jack's surprise the hen straightaway laid an egg.

But this was no ordinary egg. It was a *golden* egg! There and then Jack decided he wanted that special hen and, when he saw that the giant had fallen asleep, he jumped out of the oven, grabbed the bird and was away and running faster than greased lightning! His mother hugged him joyfully as he showed her what the little hen could do. Now they would be hungry no more!

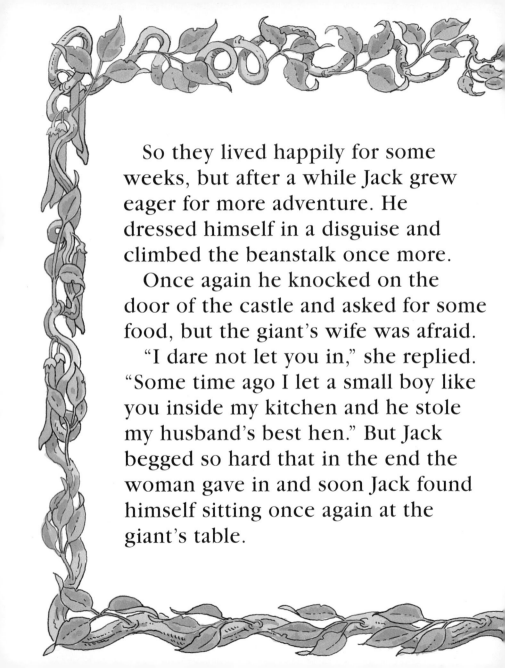

So they lived happily for some weeks, but after a while Jack grew eager for more adventure. He dressed himself in a disguise and climbed the beanstalk once more.

Once again he knocked on the door of the castle and asked for some food, but the giant's wife was afraid.

"I dare not let you in," she replied. "Some time ago I let a small boy like you inside my kitchen and he stole my husband's best hen." But Jack begged so hard that in the end the woman gave in and soon Jack found himself sitting once again at the giant's table.

In no time the giant could be heard stamping down the passage and Jack scrambled behind the wood pile.

"Bring me my money bags," he called to his wife, and soon he was happily counting his coins at the table. When he tired of his fun, he swept the money back inside the bags and fell sound asleep.

In a flash Jack grabbed the full money bags and ran from the castle. Down the beanstalk he scrambled and soon he had upturned the bags in front of his astonished mother. The golden coins flowed all over the floor and gleamed in the lamplight.

"We are rich again!" Jack laughed and he danced a jig for joy.

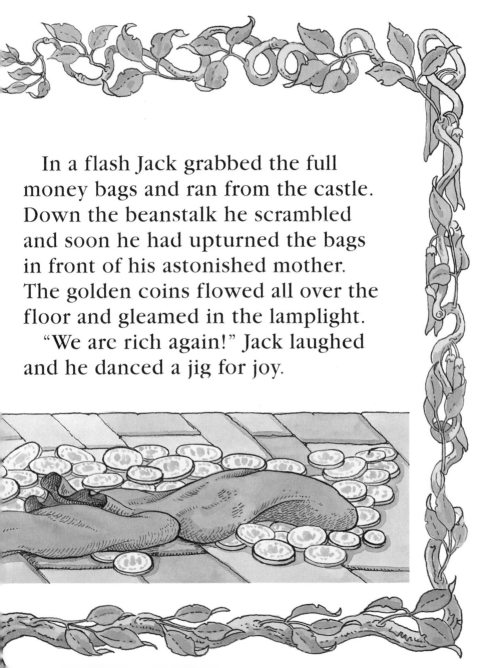

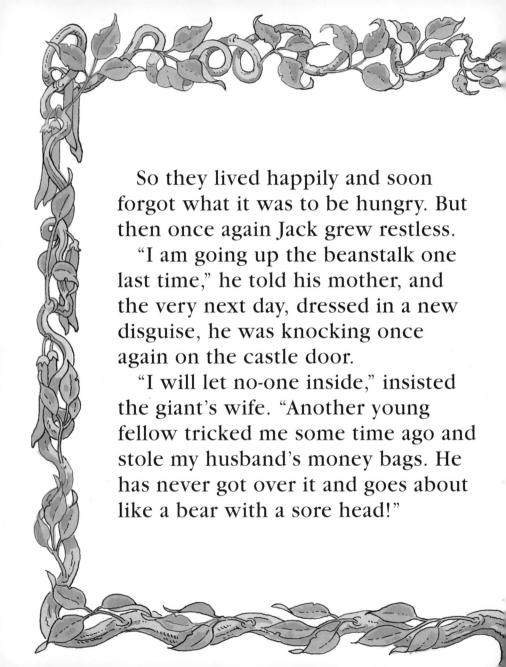

So they lived happily and soon forgot what it was to be hungry. But then once again Jack grew restless.

"I am going up the beanstalk one last time," he told his mother, and the very next day, dressed in a new disguise, he was knocking once again on the castle door.

"I will let no-one inside," insisted the giant's wife. "Another young fellow tricked me some time ago and stole my husband's money bags. He has never got over it and goes about like a bear with a sore head!"

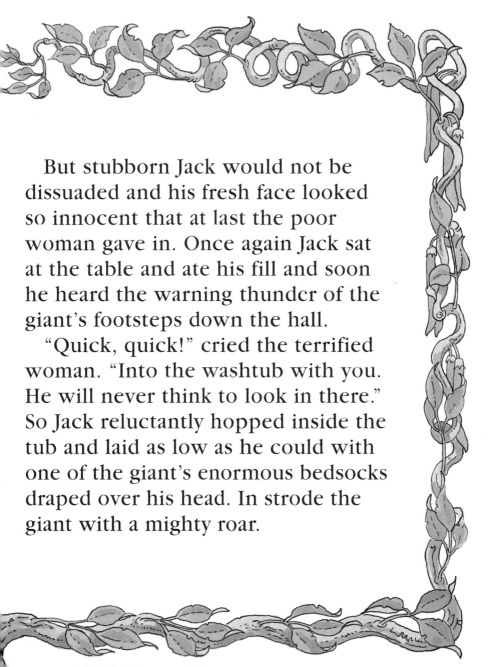

But stubborn Jack would not be dissuaded and his fresh face looked so innocent that at last the poor woman gave in. Once again Jack sat at the table and ate his fill and soon he heard the warning thunder of the giant's footsteps down the hall.

"Quick, quick!" cried the terrified woman. "Into the washtub with you. He will never think to look in there." So Jack reluctantly hopped inside the tub and laid as low as he could with one of the giant's enormous bedsocks draped over his head. In strode the giant with a mighty roar.

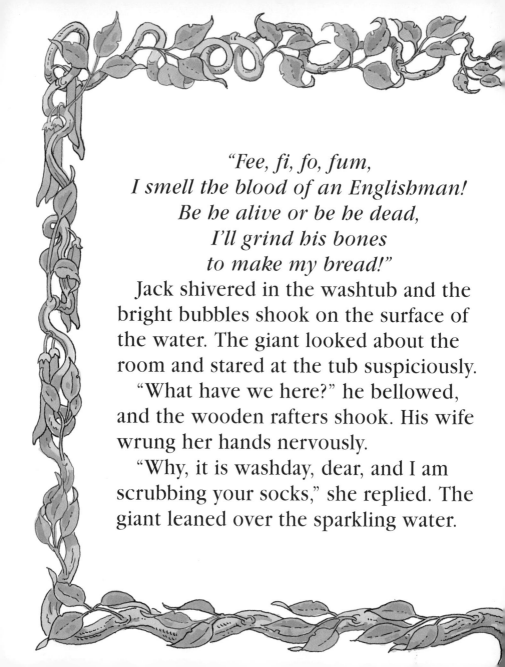

"Fee, fi, fo, fum,
I smell the blood of an Englishman!
Be he alive or be he dead,
I'll grind his bones
to make my bread!"

Jack shivered in the washtub and the bright bubbles shook on the surface of the water. The giant looked about the room and stared at the tub suspiciously.

"What have we here?" he bellowed, and the wooden rafters shook. His wife wrung her hands nervously.

"Why, it is washday, dear, and I am scrubbing your socks," she replied. The giant leaned over the sparkling water.

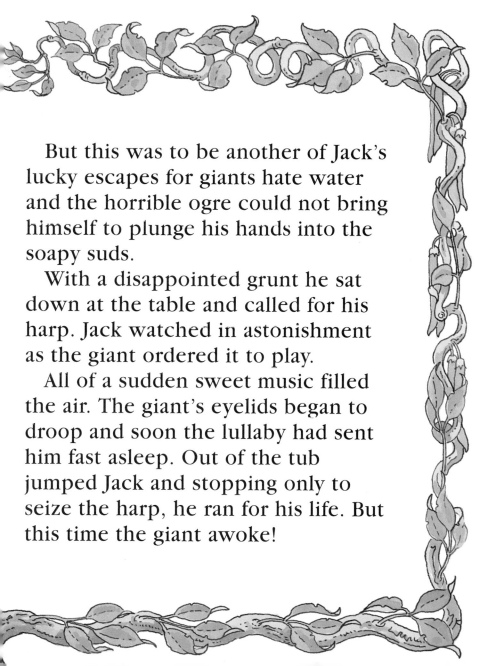

But this was to be another of Jack's lucky escapes for giants hate water and the horrible ogre could not bring himself to plunge his hands into the soapy suds.

With a disappointed grunt he sat down at the table and called for his harp. Jack watched in astonishment as the giant ordered it to play.

All of a sudden sweet music filled the air. The giant's eyelids began to droop and soon the lullaby had sent him fast asleep. Out of the tub jumped Jack and stopping only to seize the harp, he ran for his life. But this time the giant awoke!

With a howl of rage he stumbled after the boy and reached the beanstalk close behind him. As Jack slid down the stalk he could feel the giant's hot breath but the ogre could not catch the nimble Jack and soon the boy had reached the ground.

"Quick, mother! Fetch the axe!" he called. "We must chop the beanstalk!"

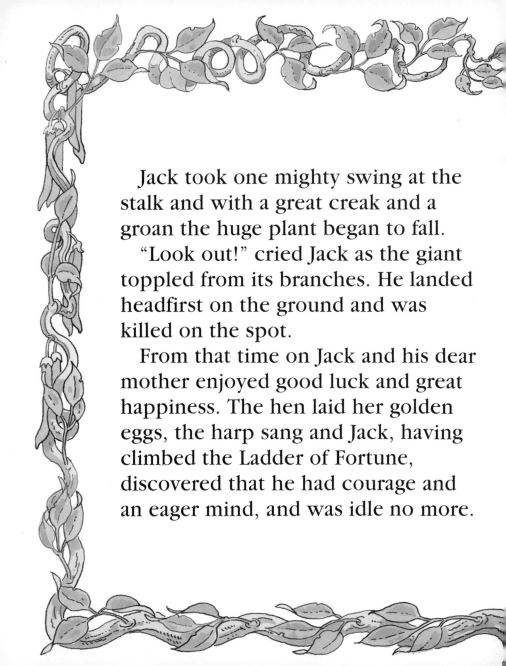

Jack took one mighty swing at the stalk and with a great creak and a groan the huge plant began to fall.

"Look out!" cried Jack as the giant toppled from its branches. He landed headfirst on the ground and was killed on the spot.

From that time on Jack and his dear mother enjoyed good luck and great happiness. The hen laid her golden eggs, the harp sang and Jack, having climbed the Ladder of Fortune, discovered that he had courage and an eager mind, and was idle no more.

JACK AND THE BEANSTALK

The earliest known reference to this old
English folk tale was in 1734 when a satirical
version was published, but the original story
must have been in existence for
generations before this time.
Jack and the Beanstalk became popular
in the early 19th century and had its first
performance as a pantomime in 1819
at Drury Lane, London.